CYNTHIA RYLANT

The Blue Hill Meadows

Illustrated by
ELLEN BEIER

A TRUMPET CLUB SPECIAL EDITION

For my mom and her much-loved dogs
—C. R.

For our "pup," Sam
—E. B.

ISBN 0-590-51187-4

Text copyright © 1997 by Cynthia Rylant.
Illustrations copyright © 1997 by Ellen Beier.
All rights reserved. Published by Scholastic Inc.,
555 Broadway, New York, NY 10012,
by arrangement with Harcourt Brace & Company.
TRUMPET and associated logos are trademarks and/or registered trademarks
of Scholastic Inc.

12 11 10 9 8 7 6 5 4 3 2 1   8 9/9 0 1 2 3/0

Printed in the U.S.A.   23

First Scholastic printing, September 1998

Contents

A Much-Loved Dog

BLUE HILL, VIRGINIA, lay in a soft green valley with blue-gray mountains and clear, shining lakes all around. It was here that the Meadow family lived—Sullivan and Eva and their boys, Willie and Ray. And it was here that they found their much-loved dog.

Actually, it was Sullivan Meadow who did the finding. Coming from work one warm summer day, he saw her wandering—a thin and weary dog—so he stopped his truck, put her inside, and took her on home.

The Meadows gave the dog some cool water and warm meat loaf and they petted away her fears. Then she curled around Sullivan's vest and slept all night long.

By morning she had a name—Lady—and Sullivan was on his way to the store for another vest.

The Meadows loved Lady like a baby. Early mornings, the oldest boy, Ray, would rise from bed to walk her outside and pet her and feed her her good-smelling breakfast.

Eva brushed Lady's fur as if Lady were a movie star and afterward rewarded her with a buttermilk biscuit.

And now and then, Sullivan had to sneak a bowl of ice cream to Lady, even though Eva had told him not to.

But it was the youngest boy, Willie, who seemed to understand Lady best of all. On warm afternoons, Willie would nap with her, his face next to hers, each breathing the breath of the other. And when Lady wanted to play, Willie knew how to be a dog for her and tug and jump and roll. Willie didn't mind being a dog and sometimes wished he could stay one a good long while.

It was Eva Meadow, being a mother herself, who first guessed that Lady had come to them carrying puppies. And when the veterinarian said yes, that Eva was right and puppies were on the way, the Meadow family started preparing. Willie was thrilled.

They first asked several families if they might want a puppy. Six families said yes. Blue Hill people loved puppies. And what else was there to do in the summer besides raise up a pup?

Sullivan and Ray built a whelping box for Lady, a quiet and safe place for her to give birth.

And Eva and Willie went to the feed store, where they bought bags of puppy food, bottles of puppy vitamins, and plenty of puppy toys.

These things done, there was nothing left to do but sit back and wait.

It was Willie who woke at dawn one morning and knew something was different. He hurried downstairs. And there in her box was Lady with a small moving thing beside her, which Willie knew must be a pup.

"Dad!" he yelled.

They all came running—Sullivan in his boxer shorts, Eva in her nightie, and Ray with a quilt around his waist.

"Are they coming? Is she having them? Is it time for the puppies?" said everyone in a flurry.

"*Yes!*" said Willie to them all.

They camped out there, the four Meadows with their dear dog, Lady, all morning long. The boys carried down blankets and pillows, Eva and Sullivan brought doughnuts and milk, and there they stayed, quiet, watchful, and thrilled.

They wanted to shout for joy each time a new puppy was born, but they didn't want to disturb Lady. Instead they threw their arms in the air and their mouths formed a silent "Hooray!" or "Yippee!" of jubilation.

Lady had seven summer puppies, all born strong and well. Six had good homes waiting for

them, and one would belong to the Meadows, a new baby for them to raise.

For many weeks there was seven times as much love in the Meadow house as before. All hours of the day someone was carrying a puppy in a blanket. The talk at mealtime was of nothing but puppies.

"You should watch the little black one," Sullivan would tell them. "He's got more vinegar in him than the rest combined. Already he's in charge of the whole family."

And on another day Eva would say, "The little brown-and-white one likes to be held the most. All she wants is a lap and a nap."

But with all the excitement and thrill of puppies, still it was Lady that Willie loved best. And he knew that she needed him especially now. As people would come and go, making a fuss over the seven lovable pups, Willie made sure he stayed close by Lady, stroking her and helping her feel as special as she'd always been. To him she was still the most beautiful dog of all.

Finally the pups went, one by one, to six good homes. When the first one left, the four Meadows stood on their front porch with tears streaming down their faces. The second was a little easier to let go. The third a little easier than the second. And by the time the sixth left, they had learned to say good-bye.

The Meadows' life returned to something like the one they'd had before all the puppies were born. But it was never exactly the same. Now there were two dogs to love. Two dogs to sleep with, to brush, to sneak ice-cream cones. There were two dog bowls and two dog beds and twice as much dog noise in the house.

Life for the Blue Hill Meadows had changed. They had a much-loved dog named Lady. And a much-loved pup named Sam.

And it was wonderful.

October Lake

I N OCTOBER IN BLUE HILL the world was so pretty it set everyone in a good mood. Houses were thick with the scent of apples bubbling on stove tops, and gardens lay ripe with the flowering of good green kale. In the front yard of the Meadow family house, a sign advertised PUMPKINS—$1 APIECE, and beside the green garage, pumpkins of every shape and personality beckoned to be set out on a front porch stoop.

October was when Sullivan Meadow liked to take a fishing trip with one of his sons, and now it

was Willie's turn. Sullivan liked to take the boys fishing one at a time ("to get to know them on their own," he'd say), and this delighted Willie. He adored Sullivan and couldn't wait to have his father all to himself.

On the morning of their big trip, Sullivan and Willie woke before dawn. They sat heavy-eyed in the kitchen, sipping on good coffee and cocoa with Willie's mother, Eva, and speaking in those soft tones people prefer in the predawn hours. Willie's older brother, Ray, lay fast asleep in the bedroom the two boys shared, unperturbed by all the excitement downstairs.

After a breakfast of boiled eggs and toast, Sullivan and Willie loaded up the pickup and headed out. The sky was blue-black, with streaks of pink dawn coming through, and Willie looked and looked at this sky but could find no words to put to it. Once Sullivan said, "My!" and that was the closest to describing it either of them came. And when they crossed over a long silver bridge, above the fog sleeping on a slow green river, Willie knew he had seen something he would never forget.

The two rode on, pulling biscuits from a basket Eva had sent and sipping on a couple of bottles of orange juice. They didn't talk much and this seemed right. The whole earth was being quiet, and they with it.

When the two finally reached Great Gap Lake, the day had lightened just enough for them to see the small, steady boats on the water. In these boats sat thoughtful fishermen, sometimes

two to a boat, but more often just one man alone. Quietly this fisherman would toss in a line, the sinker making only the faintest sound on the water: *slip*. Then he would settle himself in the boat and become still, like a heron or a crane. Still as nature itself.

Sullivan and Willie hauled their tackle and bait buckets off the bed of the pickup and headed for the little building where they could rent a boat of their own. They loaded it up with all their gear, and with one smooth push they were floating out onto the great lake.

Sullivan had never been partial to using worms for bait. He liked to use his famous recipe instead: little round balls made up of corn, honey, peanut butter, and whole wheat bread. Willie

 slid one of the balls over his hook. The bait smelled so delicious to him, he couldn't imagine any fish passing it up.

Sullivan tossed his line: *slip*. Willie tossed his: *sloop*.

Then Sullivan said to Willie, "Now, let's have some good fishing this morning, what do you say?"

And what Willie said was, "You bet."

It was a great fishing morning. The first catch was Willie's. He reeled in a seven-inch bluegill that just had to have one of those sweet-tasting balls. Across the water those thoughtful fishermen heard Sullivan say, "It's a fine one, that's for sure."

And the fishermen smiled and nodded their heads in satisfaction as if it had been themselves or one of their own boys who had caught that first fish.

Willie threw the fish back into the water, then he and Sullivan waited for another. Plenty followed. Sullivan hauled in three largemouth

bass in a row. Willie caught two sunfish. Sullivan caught one more bass and four sunfish himself. And Willie pulled in six more bluegill.

They'd remark with delight each time one of them got a bite—"Thatta boy, Willie!" or "Great going, Dad!"—and this went on all morning long until finally most of the fish around their boat had eaten as many bait balls as they were going to, and the lines stayed still, and it was time for some lunch.

They rowed back into shore and walked down the highway to a little restaurant called The Anchor. It had a big blue jukebox and the best grilled-cheese sandwiches on the face of the earth. Sullivan and Willie ordered three of these apiece, plus some barbecue potato chips, extra

pickles, and two
cold bottles of pop.
They sat together
in a dark booth,
all scrunched over,
talking and eating and

laughing for a good long time.

Sullivan told about the time he had parked his truck on a hill outside a barbershop, and as he was sitting in the barber chair getting a shave, he looked outside and saw his truck rolling backward down the hill.

"I ran to the door and yelled 'Stop!' just like it could hear me!" Sullivan said, laughing.

He described the shaving cream flying off his face as he chased down that runaway truck. Willie giggled and giggled. Willie had heard the story at least ten times before, but he always asked to hear it again. It got funnier every time.

The two sat and just talked on about things like that. Then Sullivan said they better get back to the boat. They had only a couple more hours of fishing time, and he wanted to outdo Willie's record of seven bluegill in a day.

But the fish just weren't hungry anymore. There wasn't one bite. So Sullivan rowed to a little island where he and Willie found a cool, green place to lay out of the sun, and they napped in pure contentment. Willie was feeling so happy that at first he could hardly close his eyes. But finally he drifted off and he dreamed of trees and sky and pure blue water.

On their way home that evening, Willie and Sullivan stopped at a roadside stand and bought apples and honey for Eva and peanut brittle for Ray.

Then they found a little cinder-block grocery store where they bought themselves some oat-meal cakes and chocolate milk.

They traveled on home, full of old stories and a few new ones to tell. Feeling tired and peaceful. Feeling satisfied.

It was a splendid October day.

Blizzard Party

BLUE HILL NEVER GOT much snow. It was famous for its pretty mountains but not for its snow. The town owned only one snowplow. It had just a little bit of road salt. Some folks didn't even own shovels. People there just never expected much snow.

That's why, when the weather report said eight inches of snow was coming their way, everybody went a little crazy.

The storekeepers put CLOSED signs on their shops at one in the afternoon. The beauty parlors

shut off their hair dryers and sent the ladies home to dry out naturally. The truck drivers filled up every room in the Blue Hill Motel, carrying big bags full of instant coffee and powdered dough-nuts.

And the schools called out every bus driver in Blue Hill and sent all the children home early.

Willie Meadow was one of the children who was supposed to get on one of these buses. He should have found Bus 12, climbed up its steps, and ridden it all the way back to the little white house where his mother, Eva, and his father, Sullivan, were waiting for him. Eva was baking a cherry pie. Sullivan was digging around in the green garage for something he might turn into a sled. And Willie's big brother, Ray, was already climb- ing off the high school bus in front of the house, whistling for joy. A blizzard was com- ing, and everyone was excited.

At the elementary school, Willie knew what his bus number was and he knew where the bus parked every day. He had never had any trouble finding that bus.

But this blizzard day was different. Some bus drivers got to the school before other drivers could, and the buses got parked in different places. Willie stood on the sidewalk, wind and snow whipping his face, his ears hurting because he'd lost his hat, and he couldn't find Bus 12. It wasn't in its usual place. It wasn't pulling out and it wasn't pulling in. He got scared. Everyone was leaving and everything was moving fast. A blizzard—something he'd never seen in his life—was coming. And he couldn't find his bus.

With tears in his eyes, Willie ran back inside the school. He would find his teacher, Mr. Theodore, and Mr. Theodore would help him find his bus. But when he finally found Mr. Theodore and they finally got back outside to search for Bus 12, all of the buses were gone. All of them. Everything was silent. The snow was coming down harder, Bus 12 had disappeared, and Willie Meadow was stranded at the edge of a blizzard.

Willie's eyes began to fill up again, and that was when he heard Mr. Theodore say, "Well, we'll just have a blizzard party at my house."

Willie wiped his eyes and he followed Mr. Theodore inside to phone Sullivan and Eva. The next thing Willie knew he was riding in Mr. Theodore's Volkswagen and listening to a song about somebody named Peggy Sue. The snow was thick and the wheels of the little car spun. Mr. Theodore

drove very slowly. Willie wished more than any-thing that he could be home with his father and mother and his brother, Ray. But home was fif-teen miles away, while Mr. Theodore's house was only one mile away, and in this blizzard, Willie felt ready to call any place home.

Willie liked Mr. Theodore. He had never had a teacher who kept a hedgehog in his class-room. Or who brought genuine moon rocks for his students to touch. Or who tried to grow trees out of avocado pits. Mr. Theodore was the strangest teacher Willie had ever had. And Willie thought the world of him.

So it was a little scary for Willie, going to Mr. Theodore's house. To be in a teacher's kitch-en or living room seemed as impossible to Willie as being on Mars. He wasn't sure which idea was more exciting: the mounting blizzard or Mr. Theodore's house.

Mr. Theodore talked nonstop all the way. "This is so great, Willie. A blizzard. Amazing! Right here in Blue Hill. Can you believe it?"

And he rolled down his window so they could feel the snow on their faces. Mr. Theodore said he loved snow even more than he loved sunshine. "If we lived in Alaska it would be just snow," he told Willie. "Here, it's *gold*."

Willie smiled. Maybe Mr. Theodore's house wouldn't be so scary after all.

When they finally arrived and walked into the house, the living room was just jumping with cats. Willie walked in the door and they were

everywhere. And there
was a parrot in a cage.
A turtle in a tub.
An iguana crawling
around an aquarium.

   Mr. Theodore smiled.
   "Future third grade
visitors," he said.

He led Willie into the
kitchen, which had a
wall full of windows
and a clock shaped
like a giraffe and a wife
Mr. Theodore called Rebecca. Willie felt shy,
but Rebecca gave him a
cup of hot chocolate,
a bowl of corn
chips, and a hug.
He began to feel terrific.

By the time a pair of headlights cut through Mr. Theodore's driveway, and Sullivan, Eva, and Ray all piled out of the truck, Willie was running around outside Mr. Theodore's big yellow house in the middle of a snowball fight. Willie had forgotten to miss them, forgotten to long for his little white house. It wasn't until he saw the faces of his family that he was reminded he wasn't home.

Mr. Theodore and Rebecca invited them all inside to wait out the blizzard. Willie's father was worried and said that they should try to get back home right away. But Ray saw the telescope in the second-story window, and Eva saw the five cats all lined up at the picture window, and they both talked Sullivan into staying.

Blizzards always get worse before they get better. The Meadow family was in the big yellow house a long time. They played slapjack and rummy. They watched a whale movie. They made peanut-butter cookies. And they petted cats every minute they were there.

When finally the wind died down and they saw there wasn't so much snow after all, the Meadows piled back into their truck and waved good-bye to Mr. Theodore and Rebecca. Willie watched them as he rode away home, watched Mr. Theodore give Rebecca a hug and walk on back into that big yellow house full of cats. And he knew why Mr. Theodore was such a good teacher. Mr. Theodore was happy.

Willie went on home with his family, home where a sled rigged up from an old washing machine lid, and some sweet cherry pie, sat waiting for him.

Then for what remained of that day, he played in a snow he had waited so many years to see.

A Perfect Gift

SPRING IN THE LITTLE TOWN of Blue Hill was always full of flowers. Eva Meadow, who was herself raising up two boys who grew like weeds in the sun, thought that life could not be better when on those lovely May mornings she planted her petunias around the small white house and the green garage and the faithful old cherry tree she loved so well.

This particular May, as Eva was carrying her flowers about the yard, her son Willie had her very much on his mind. Each morning he watched as she moved and hummed and talked to their dear dogs, Lady and Sam, and he wondered what, of all the things in the world, would make her happy.

Mother's Day was coming. Mr. Theodore at school had reminded him again and again and so many times that Willie had nearly come to believe it the most important day on earth. As a result, he was feeling a great responsibility. He believed he must find for his mother the perfect gift.

But he did not know how.

Willie's older brother, Ray, always gave their mother the same gift each year: he made her a new pencil holder. Eva Meadow hoped to be a writer someday when her children were raised and out the door, and knowing this, a few years back Ray had made a pencil holder from a coffee can. Willie had thought the gift rather dreary and uninteresting, but Eva had gone on and on about it so much that Ray seemed almost afraid to ever give her anything else. So for three years in a row now he had given her pencil

holders. She would put the old one in her trunk, place the new one on her small desk, and she would say, "Now, *this* one will bring me the luck I need." And she would give Ray a kiss on the forehead.

Willie had paid so
little attention to the
gifts he had given
on Mother's Day
that he could not
even remember
them now. But this
year he could think only
of one thing: he must give his
mother a gift that meant something.

For many days Willie watched his mother
with great interest. His father, Sullivan, noticed
this and one day took his son aside. "Something
troubling you, Willie?" his father asked.

Willie shook his head. He wasn't ready yet to
admit that he could not think of an extraordinary
gift for his mother. Willie did not want his father
to know this about his youngest son: that he had
no talent for inspiration.

One night Willie and Ray lay in the dark in their room, each staring out at the bright white moon hanging solemnly outside their window. Because Ray had enjoyed such good fortune a few years back, hitting on the very thing Eva Meadow seemed to want most in the world—pencil holders that brought her luck—Willie decided to ask Ray if he'd had any other revelations about their mother. Maybe Ray knew her in a different way. Maybe he knew what else a mother with a lucky pencil holder might need.

"Have you made Mom her pencil holder yet?" Willie asked Ray in a friendly way, hoping to soften him into talking. Ray was not much of a talker.

"Yep," answered Ray.

"Is it nice?" Willie asked.

"Yep," Ray answered again.

"I don't know what I'm getting her," Willie said. "Any ideas?"

"Nope," answered Ray, who turned on his side and began to snore.

Willie lay awake a long time. He was hoping for a revelation. But the perfect gift did not reveal itself to him that night, nor the night after, nor the night after that. But finally, and luckily, just two days before Mother's Day, Willie Meadow realized what he could give his mother, Eva.

He had woken early in the morning, feeling rather desperate and full of worry. He shuffled

into the kitchen for some
cereal, and there he
saw his mother
standing at the
window, rapt
and breathless.
Outside, a large
wild rabbit was
sitting beneath
her cherry tree.
And when Willie
saw the look on his mother's face, he knew what
he must do for her.

He must get her that rabbit.

Wild rabbits are not easy to catch. They
want to be free and they
use their wits to stay that
way. But Willie wasn't
interested in catching

the rabbit. His mother would
not want a rabbit in
a cage.

Willie was
interested in
making the rabbit
stay, in making Eva's cherry tree the most wonderful place in the world for a rabbit to be.

And Willie thought he knew how to do it.

So, when Mother's Day morning came, Eva
Meadow rose early from bed as usual, put on
her robe, and quietly padded into the kitchen to
start Sunday coffee brewing. And as always, she
glanced out the window to see if the wild rabbit
had come back to the cherry tree. She hoped to
see that lovely sight again.

But this morning what Eva Meadow saw was
a far lovelier sight than a wild brown rabbit.
She saw her own boy Willie kneeling beneath

that tree, trowel in hand, pouring seeds into the earth he had overturned. All around him in a circle were little signs marking those seeds he had already planted: ALFALFA. CARROTS. RADISHES. LETTUCE.

Eva pushed open the screen door.

Willie smiled. "Happy Mother's Day, Mom."

Eva hugged him so hard he thought his bones might pop. And as she did, from the edge of the pine woods, a pair of curious brown eyes was watching them, waiting for the most delicious garden a wild rabbit might ever hope for.

The illustrations in this book were done in watercolor
and liquid acrylic on Arches hot-press paper.
The display type was set in Goudy Italian Old Style Italic.
The text type was set in Goudy.
Designed by Linda Lockowitz